CAMBO

HUSTLE

J. LEE PORTER

&

ED TEJA

This story was previously published as

A Calculated Gamble

NEW IN TOWN

"If you don't gamble, you'll never win."

— *Aldous Huxley*

I stepped out into the warm night a little after eleven, walking away from the room I'd rented at a small guesthouse near the riverfront. I walked away from the Tonle Sap, heading down a street filled with girlie bars. The waterfront in Phnom Penh, the capital of Cambodia, boasts a lot of nightlife but tonight that wasn't what had me hitting the streets.

It was still early for the area. Things were just getting started. The bars had spilled out into the street the way they do at night, with the proprietors setting up tables outside their establishments, and the bar girls, dressed in tight shorts or short skirts and halter tops, taking their places. Walking those streets was a bit like walking a gauntlet. The girls, prowling for prey, the neon lights, the music charged the atmosphere and gave the very air edge. Whenever a man walked by, one or more girls would begin their long-range assault, waving and calling out encouragements, urging him to come into their bar and buy them a drink. All of their words, their movements, promised the lucky man with some ready cash a sexy and fun evening. All he had to do was enter their lair.

The street was alive — loud and raucous, projecting a scene that would look right in an old movie but with the vibrancy of a carnival sideshow. The girls, needing to make money, played the role of show barkers, doing their best to make it seem that everyone inside was having a boisterous good time. "Step inside, touch the naked ladies."

Walking by at a steady pace earned me disappointed cries and a few insults born of frustration and desperation. Few of the girls chose the career of a bar girl and would prefer to get on with the night's work, earn their money, and get it over with. I have nothing against those places, but that evening, I was headed for a specific destination — a particular bar among these so-similar venues, that boasted with the strange name of <u>SNAKE GIRL</u>. In a place where most of the bar names implied sex or hot females one way or another, it seemed odd. The bar I was walking by, which a neon sign informed me was called <u>HOT PUSSY</u>, at least made some sense. But SNAKE GIRL?

Perhaps that was the point — to stand out however it could.

The girls along my route offered the usual mix of ages and beauty, or a lack of either quality. The majority of the girls had delicious brown skin, but the miracle of modern hairstyling meant I saw the gamut of blondes, redheads, and whatever it is you call girls with purple or green hair. Even the ones who had that lovely lustrous black hair I associate with Asia, had it cut in a variety of styles that were probably modeled after Western movie stars. I wouldn't know much about them — movie stars, I mean.

While they waited for lonely customers to stop in and appease their thirst and lust, the girls sat in plastic chairs in front of the bars. They idled the time away, playing with their cell phones, calling out to passing men, and eating noodle dishes, all the while chatting nonstop with each other.

If you are going to play the bar girl game, buying the girls the special, overpriced, nonalcoholic lady drinks so that they will spend time with you, whether you want to screw them or just have some company, Phnom Penh is an inexpensive place to do it.

A man could do worse than to sit with a girl, getting to know her. And if you are looking for more than company, getting to know her a little is probably a decent investment. It lets you know what she's like before you pay the fee that management gets to let her leave, her bar fine, and take her home.

That worked for the girls too. Even if she didn't strike your fancy and you moved on to another, at least she earned something from her cut from the drinks. It wouldn't thrill her that you passed on the idea of spending the night or even a short time with her, but she could feel she hadn't totally wasted her time. With the financial incentive plain and out in the open, the girls were eager to compete for prospective clients. And that was exactly what the bar owners wanted, too.

I walked the few blocks of this amazing yellow brick road of the night world, smiling and nodding at the girls while ignoring the cries of "buy me a drink," until I came to it —SNAKE GIRL Bar. Wedged in between BAD GIRL BAR and PUSSY PALACE, it was small and didn't stand out and it seemed odd that one girl sat outside, alone. She was on the phone, texting happily, but made the effort to get up to follow me inside.

I made my way straight to the bar and took a seat next to a girl wearing tight shorts and a tighter Black Sabbath tee-shirt that emphasized her breasts. "Slow night?" I asked as I sat.

She glanced up to stare at me, giving me a feeble smile that stunk of sullen hopelessness. I wanted to see that smile blossom. Her lovely brown face looked wrong with that look on it. Her mouth opened slightly as she started to say something, then she changed her mind.

She glared at the girl who had followed me in. I suppose it was a territorial glare because the other girl turned and, staring at her phone, went back outside.

"Help you?" the bartender asked, emerging from the back. He had a noticeable German accent.

"I'll have a whiskey, something Western, please. The local shit almost killed me once."

"The local shit is shite." He chuckled at his own joke. "I've got Jack, if that's okay?"

"Jack Daniels is fine. Let me buy you one, too."

He grinned. "Thanks."

I nodded toward the girl. "Give our Lady of Perpetual Sadness here a lady drink."

He nodded and grinned at her. "Chatty Kathy, you are in luck."

"You nice," she said, brightening.

"I am at that," I said. "And I am also terribly modest, which makes me even nicer."

Her puzzled look pleased me. Undeterred, but encouraged by the glass of colored water and the token the bartender gave her, she began stroking my leg. Clearly, I'd miscalculated. By rewarding her for being indifferent to me, I'd encouraged her to do exactly what I'd wanted to avoid. Live and learn... or was the appropriate saying: "no good deed goes unpunished"?

The bartender was watching me. "What kind of name is Chatty Kathy?" I asked him.

He grinned. "A nickname. Westerners can't or don't want to bother saying her Khmer name."

"Chanthavy," she said.

"Rather than stumble over it, they renamed her Chatty Kathy. They thought it was funny and it stuck."

"Chanthavy means 'as beautiful as the moon'," she said as the bartender poured us each a whiskey. She flashed a seductive smile that totally ruined an attempt at an aloof expression.

I tore my eyes away to speak to the bartender. "And your name is Becker, right?"

Surprise flickered over his face, then he smiled. "It means 'as macho as the sun'," he said. "Do I know you?"

"No, sorry. Arnold in Penang told me to look you up," I said.

"Arnold? Which Arnold?" he asked, giving me a blank smile.

"The Arnold you owe fifty bucks."

"Me, skip on a debt?"

"He said you never paid your share for some whores and dope you two enjoyed last March."

He scowled. "Oh, that Arnold in Penang. The man's got a memory, that's for sure."

"Hey, it's about sex and money."

"You aren't American."

"Dutch," I said.

"Then you aren't Arnold's cousin, Dudley. I was afraid—"

"No. I'm Aaron... someone who met him at the Rouge in Penang."

"Is he still dealing blackjack?"

I laughed. "If Arnold were dealing cards, it wouldn't be at the Rouge. No, he is still pimping out of that room over the old lady's store."

The German grinned. I'd passed his test. "I don't have his money if that's why you're here. This dump doesn't pay for shit so it will be some time before he gets it."

"No. I'm not after your money. Arnold owed me a favor. When I found out I was going to be here for a bit, I asked him who he knew. He said you were the only person he knew in Phnom Penh who knows where things happen."

"Things? That's a broad term." He nodded at Chatty Kathy. "You got girls right here."

"I'm looking for a poker game."

His eyes narrowed. "Well, you are in luck, moron. We've got an entire fucking casino across town. It's called Naga World. It will be the delight of any tuk tuk driver on the street to take you to their front door."

Another whore, with red and green hair cut in a sculpted diagonal, walked up and put her hand on my shoulder. The one stroking my leg glared at her but said nothing. I gave her a smile and sipped my drink.

I looked at Becker. "I mean quiet games. Private ones. The games where people lose their money quietly, drink quietly, and then lose more money."

"Quietly," he said.

"I'm thinking of places that don't involve people with guns or houses that take a huge cut of the pot."

"Boy, you are fucking picky." He grinned. "I'm not sure such places exist in Asia." He refilled the drinks. "Arnold sent you to me?"

"I made him. He owed me. I'm a professional poker player and I want to find a game."

He nodded. "Why in Phnom Penh? They have better games in Penang."

I sighed. If I expected his help, it seemed I was going to have to tell him everything. Not that my reasons were secret, just embarrassing. "I hadn't planned to come here at all and now I'm winging it. My departure was rather hasty and totally unplanned."

"Rushing is a bad idea. A person needs plans."

"My plan is to play a big poker game in Singapore a month from now. It's an invitational and the buy-in is big by my standards. I need to play it, partly because it's hard to get on that list of players. In Penang, I was playing steadily so that I could raise enough money for the buy-in."

"Makes sense."

"After a game the other days, some guy, I don't even know who, turned out to be a sore loser. Unfortunately, he was a well-connected sore loser. He decided to take out his bad fortune on me, personally by sending some thugs after me. I got tipped off. I managed to get out with my bag before they grabbed me. I went to see Arnold for contacts. You were the only name in Phnom Penh he could give me."

Becker considered that. "So, what do you need a name for?"

"To find more games. Shelling out for an extra plane ticket and entry visa, plus abandoning a room I'd paid for in advance emptied my wallet. Not that I'm low on money, but because things unraveled so fast, so suddenly, I'm short on ready cash."

"But you have money."

"Yes, but not enough for that big game. I had a way to go before I finished accumulating my stake. So now I need to get going on that again. I'd also like to earn enough to cover living expenses here for a few days. I'm meeting people in Vientiane in a week and my visa for Laos isn't good until then."

"How are you going to play a game without money?

It was a valid question. "I've got money. It's just that I'm hesitant to convert my assets to dollars just to cover living expenses. They dropped recently and will come back up, but for now —"

"You have to pay for essentials like booze and whores," he said.

"Right."

"This is just being nosy, but what kind of assets do you have?"

"Cryptocurrency. Bitcoin."

"Another gamble," he laughed.

"A calculated risk. I approach poker and investing the same way — rationally. I try to use skill and trust luck only when necessary. Part of my long-term strategy has been to convert my winnings into Bitcoin, just holding back what I need for current expenses. That keeps my wealth safe and transportable. Under normal circumstances, when I need money for travel and to pay bills, I wait for the Bitcoin price to peak and sell enough to live on for a time."

"And that does what?"

"If things go my way, over the long haul the value of Bitcoin keeps going up relative to dollars. It doesn't always do it in the short term, of course. There aren't any sure things. But I did my research and think that if I'm patient, one day I'll be able to live off it."

"Live off it?" Becker shook his head. Disbelief was heavy. "How the hell do you live off something like that? From what I hear it's just computer code."

"It's a secure blockchain. Without getting into it deeply, it's just computer code used to create a ledger. Outwardly it's no different than the one that gives you your bank balance, but it's private and safer."

Becker laughed. "I couldn't live off my bank balance."

"No, because they pay you crap interest and they store your money in dollars or euros. Those don't have any investment value and can't actually appreciate except one compared to the other. And as long as governments keep printing more, over time you'll lose the value. Bitcoin is a finite resource. That makes it more like gold or silver, except I can sell it or move it around easily on a memory stick or over the Internet."

"No shit?"

I smiled. "It works like this. Say I save ten thousand dollars and buy Bitcoin. If I'm right, and other people decide it's a good investment, by the time I need it, it's worth one hundred thousand. And if I save a hundred thousand... you get the idea. But this has been a rocky year, to say the least, and now, when I needed cash, the price was down. You can't live for long off the principle if you are taking advantage of depreciation — the math just doesn't work out. A professional poker player is nothing if not someone who trusts math."

"But you put too much in Bitcoin."

I nodded. "In hindsight, I got too eager and depleted my emergency fund. If I'd known I was going to leave Penang when I did, I'd have held back some cash."

"So, you need a big deal game?"

"Ideally."

While Becker considered what he was willing to tell me, the whore behind me spotted a guy walking to a table outside the bar.

Her hand slipped from my shoulder, and she rushed over to him, leaving a cloud of cheap perfume in her wake. I wasn't much fun and Chatty Kathy hadn't relinquished her claim.

"I haven't been here that long," Becker said. "Over time, like a hotel concierge, I usually do get to know who is doing what in a town, but right now, I can't do much for you."

Chatty Kathy let her hand move up my leg to a more intimate place. I assumed she thought I was ignoring her. I had been, but I wasn't now.

Experience had taught her well. With a heterosexual male, her attention-getting strategy was rather foolproof. I looked at her and she sighed. "Mr. Chan's," she said. "Every Wednesday he has a poker game for some Excellencies."

"Excellencies?" I asked.

The German laughed. "She means VIPs — rich Khmer fucks. The Khmer call anyone who might be important an excellency. I think that's just in case they really are important. They might get insulted if you don't know who they are."

"Yes," Chatty Kathy said. "It is important not to insult them. They can make big trouble. Bad trouble is bad."

"So, the excellencies play poker for big stakes on Wednesday... and this is Sunday." That gave me time to make something happen. "Do you know where the game is?" I asked.

She frowned, sizing me up. "It's for excellencies."

"Could you get me into it? I want to play."

She scowled as if she thought she might see into me; I saw intelligence in those eyes that I felt sure she'd been masking. "You need plenty money to buy into a high-stakes game like Chan's."

"If I had the money, though... could you do it?"

She made a sour face. "Chan doesn't let unknown people in. You need a sponsor."

Becker, the German, rubbed his chin. "I'd forgotten about that game. Chan keeps it exclusive. Lots of security." He looked toward the door. "Are you any fucking good at the game?"

"Yes," I said, again exercising my famous modesty. "I'm exceptionally good. Why?"

"I won't even charge you for this information, because it is small beer, but tomorrow night there's a small game," Becker said. He nodded at Chatty Kathy. "Wang's is tomorrow, right?"

"Chinese monster Wang," she snorted. "Sure."

"Chinese monster Wang? Curious name. Is he a bad guy?"

She laughed and held her hands up, palms facing each other, about eight inches apart. "Not bad. Big."

"I hear that Wang likes to get _barang_ into his game if they've got the buy-in," the bartender said.

"Barang?"

"Foreigners. He thinks having expat money at the table will pull in a few richer Khmer. Everyone wants to move up."

"But the stakes are low?"

He nodded. "It's an introduction to the local scene. You might meet someone who knows of a bigger game and is willing to make introductions. And, if you win a little money to cover expenses while meeting people, it's all to the good."

He was right, and it sounded promising. Even if I only won enough to meet my immediate needs, I'd be playing poker.

"That sounds like a decent idea." I smiled at Kathy and ordered another round. When my self-appointed date pressed her body against me, I asked her outright. "Can you get me in Wang's poker game tomorrow night?"

She considered it. "Yes. If you have five thousand. Can do."

Getting that much wasn't a serious problem. I could get a cash advance on my credit card. If the cards were good, I could pay it back immediately. "I can get it tomorrow."

She smiled and rubbed my crotch. "Then tonight we go make love."

"We do?"

"I like you. You pay me for a long time. Tomorrow you get money and at night I take you to Wang's. If you win, I get fifty dollars. Extra."

Becker and I laughed. "She's a tough negotiator," the German said. "I should point out that if you keep her for a couple of days, it's only fair that you pay her bar fine for both nights."

I doubted anyone in the history of hiring bar girls had ever done that, but Becker was covering his ass. It wasn't that much money, and if it earned me a friend in Phnom Penh, it was a bargain.

I liked cultivating good contacts and I never knew when I'd be back in Phnom Penh again. "Fair enough. I can handle that."

Chatty Kathy, now happy Chatty Kathy, let her hands get familiar with my terrain.

"You ready to go?" I asked. "We stop for dinner on the way."

"Buy me another drink first," she said.

"You haven't finished that one," I pointed out.

"I'm not thirsty."

"So why buy another drink?"

"Getting you to buy me drinks is the job I do when we are in the bar."

The German was grinning at me as I dug out my wallet. He found the education the girl was providing me amusing. Arguing with Chatty Kathy wasn't smart or profitable.

"She eats like a horse," he warned me.

"Good food too," she said. "No junk."

"She's not the cheapest date," Becker said, sounding like the voice of experience.

"Seems not." I gave myself a moment to savor the irony that I was spending money on a whore, food, and booze when what I wanted was to build my stake. But you have to spend money to make any. It was a calculated gamble.

WANG'S GAME

The next day, after breakfast and a trip to the bank, we sat in rattan chairs on a restaurant patio on the Riverfront while Chatty Kathy made a couple of calls. Khmer is a musical language and made no sense to my ear.

"Okay," she said when she hung up. "Wang says you can play if you got cash and I work."

"Work?"

She wrinkled her nose. "Chinese monster Wang needs a waitress for the game. He doesn't pay good, but gamblers tip okay." She ran her tongue slowly over her lips. "You won't need me until after it is over."

It was a good plan. It would keep her out of my hair while I played. As a bonus, her being the waitress could be useful to me. "Will you be the only waitress?"

"Of course. Chinese monster Wang too cheap to have more than one. And he tends bar himself because he doesn't trust people."

"Then, when I am playing, I'll order whisky."

She grinned. "But you don't want whisky."

"I want a clear head. Bring me ginger ale and bitters. Will Chinese monster Wang keep that a secret?"

She rubbed her fingers together. "Twenty is plenty for him to mind his own business," she said, chuckling. I could see that my asking represented an opportunity and Miss Entrepreneur of the Year didn't hesitate to take advantage of it. Still, I handed her a twenty. That earned me a laugh. "You know everyone does that. Yes?"

She was right.

That night, after dinner, she led me on a meandering walk through the dark back streets and alleys of Phnom Penh. I would never have found the place on my own, but she knew exactly where to go.

When we arrived, we climbed outside stairs to a room above a shop where some people were setting up for the game. She introduced me to Wang, an overweight Chinese man with a greasy smile. "She says you good player," he informed me and pointing at Chatty Kathy.

"An enthusiastic player, at least," I said. "What is the game?"

His fat face wrinkled in a smile. "In Wang's place, we only play five-card draw."

"I'd prefer Texas Hold'em."

"That game is popular in some places around the city," he said. "Not here." His dismissive tone made it clear that I was free to go to any of those inferior places.

"Five-card draw is fine," I said as a slim and lithe Cambodian girl came walking up to us.

"Sophi," Wang told me. "She is the dealer."

I gave her the long, lingering look she deserved. Sophi filled out a Chinese Chong Sam like it had been poured on. This was my idea of classic Asian sexy. But she was all business.

Wang opened a small lockbox and gave it to her. She put it on the table, then got a cup of tea before sitting down and opening the box. It held ten or twenty sealed decks of cards. She examined them and put two decks on the table, then returned the rest in the box. She checked the chips and folded her hands on the table.

When we sat down at the table, there were four other players: a bald Brit in a stained tee-shirt, a well-dressed Cambodian who introduced himself as Chea Pran, and two other young Cambodian men in shirts and slacks.

As we each handed Wang the cash for our buy-in, Sophi slid a neat stack of chips to sit in front of us.

I can't say much about most of the players in the game. None of them was there to socialize really, so there wasn't a lot of chatting, although the Brit and I bantered a little about the upcoming World Cup. Spain had just beaten the Netherlands badly, and naturally, he wanted to rub that in.

Chatty Kathy took our order for overpriced drinks and when she'd served them, we got down to business.

Sophi opened a sealed deck, took out the jokers, and shuffled it seven times, as professionally as I've seen in any casino. Then the Brit cut, she burned a card and dealt the hand.

The opening salvos were muted. I like to lay back a bit in the beginning and get a feel for styles, but none of the four seemed to have much of a method to his playing.

I tossed in a few hands early on, willing to pay to see which of the other players liked to push his luck and who didn't trust the cards.

Once I settled in, I started winning. The two Cambodians in suits were easy to bluff and made it far too easy to tell when they had a decent hand.

From the way he played, I figured the Brit was there because he enjoyed the game. He stuck with a few hands I'm sure I would have folded, but he was smart enough that he only did it when it was a cheap bet. He stretched out his money.

Chea Pran was the only one who appeared to have anything close to deep pockets. Unfortunately for him, he had no card sense. A truly rotten poker player and frequently reckless, he relied on luck to take care of the trivial tasks like filling inside straights.

It was fun to watch him try to maintain a poker face of some sort. When he looked at his hand and a thin smile flickered over his lips, I figured it was time for some fun.

Earlier, he'd been dealt two pair at this point and he'd smiled then too, but this was a different smile, a new tell. I was guessing he had three of a kind.

That would have been a problem, but I had three aces.

When Chea Pran made a healthy bet, I was certain he had three, and that they were probably face cards.

After a furious bit of swearing directed at his cards, the Brit dropped out. He'd gotten stuck with a hand that had what we call "potential." Maybe a possible straight. He didn't have the guts or money to find out if his cards could live up to their potential, which was probably smart.

One of the other Khmer players dropped out too, but the other grimaced and stayed in.

Chea Pran threw in two cards, and when the dealer sent him two new ones, he picked them up and a beautiful smile lit up Chea Pran's face — a look of delight let us know that his dreams had been answered.

Compared to the first smile when we were dealt the cards, this was the sun going supernova. In short, he was acting.

I took one card, to keep everyone guessing. The other Khmer took three.

Chea Pran bid a hundred dollars.

I raised him another hundred.

The other Khmer clearly hadn't gotten his wishes fulfilled and threw in his hand. Leaving just the two of us.

Chea Pran studied my face, studied his cards, studied the pot in the middle of the table, and then ordered a drink. I smiled. He was sweating. While he waited for his drink, which was gin and tonic, he studied the same three things again, in the same order — my face, his cards, the great stack of chips in the pot.

After taking a sip of the drink that Chatty Kathy handed him, he raised me another hundred.

"So much study deserves a reward," I said, and I called.

My three aces beat his three queens.

I raked in the pot and Chea Pran sighed. "That's it, for me," he said.

The Brit was pushing his chair back too. "I'm done," he said.

The two other Khmer players blinked but said nothing. Wang cashed us in, and the Brit and the suited Cambodians slipped away. "I need a drink," I said.

"I'll buy," Chea Pran said.

Chatty Kathy poured me a whisky.

I looked around. "Everyone is going home," I said.

Chea Pran nodded. "Wang is in no rush to close."

Chinese monster Wang unsmilingly nodded. I'd call his look inscrutable but pleased. Chatty Kathy was cleaning things off the table and Sophi was putting the unopened decks back in the lockbox.

I graciously sipped the drink.

"You are skilled at poker," Chea Pran said.

"I always like hearing that," I said. "Too bad the take-home pay wasn't better."

He scrunched his face up. "The others didn't bring much money for you to win... or they decided to take it home with them. They could tell you were too good for them."

"I was lucky tonight." I was being careful, not humble. Somehow, the idea that you are skillful at poker all too easily gets misconstrued into the idea that you are cheating. Being good suggests an unfair advantage. I suspect that is because no one wants to think that they could play better if they took the time to learn.

He waved a hand. "There are better games in town if you want to win serious money," he said. "I'm not good enough to risk them, myself." He laughed uneasily. "You showed me that much this evening."

"As much as I like the idea, cash is a bit short at the moment." I held up the few hundred I'd won. "Even if I had a connection and could get invited to a game like that, I don't think this will be nearly enough to get me in."

"No," he said. "But the point being, you would like to play in a game where the players are better and the stakes higher?"

"Especially if they were playing Texas Hold-em."

Chea Pran stood and handed Wang some dollars. "Can we meet for breakfast?" he asked me. "I need to do some checking, but I might have a proposition for you."

"I have one for you tonight," Chatty Kathy said.

"A late breakfast would be good. More of a brunch."

"Where are you staying?" I told him. "I will send a car for you. Would ten be all right?"

"Perfect."

Then as Kathy led me back through the winding corridors of the back streets, I found myself wondering what this rich man wanted from a poker player.

"He is an excellency," she told me. "Or wants to be one."

"What could he want?"

"Something that will make him richer or more powerful," she said, her voice flat. "He will gain something from whatever it is."

"Am I making a mistake by talking to him?"

She laughed. "How can you get ahead except by letting the powerful people use you? Just make sure you are well paid for doing his bidding. What else matters?"

Her worldview was amazingly consistent and free of any irony. When you were born into the bottom of the heap, you did what it took to climb higher. If that helped someone else's agenda, what difference did that make? She was helping me out because it suited her. It was good for business. That meant she had no more guilt about being a whore than I did when I took some chump's money from him.

You didn't survive life by worrying too much about the other person. Kathy and I shared that view. You didn't cheat people, you didn't take what wasn't yours, but you couldn't worry about the consequences of other people's decisions.

Maybe Mother Theresa did, but then I read that the woman had an incredible ego herself. Kathy and I did too, but I was sure that's where the similarities ended.

"We stop and get food, then a bottle of whisky to take to your room," she said.

Kathy was either a great actress or she loved her work. At the end of the day, it was likely a mixture of the two. No one said you had to be totally consistent or all one or the other. And the balance of that mix didn't matter much when we got to my bed.

AN OFFER TO REFUSE

A dark SUV picked us up in front of my guesthouse the next morning, right on time. The burly, overdressed Khmer man with dark glasses got out and stared for a moment before walking over to where Chatty Kathy sitting at the outside table with me. "I'm here to pick you up," he said.

I didn't feel like playing nice. "Picking us up."

He went rigid. "My instructions are to bring you — just you," he said.

"Then you were told incorrectly," I said. "She hasn't had breakfast yet either."

"Just you," he said stubbornly.

I gave him my most cheerful smile. "Sorry. I understood the invitation to include my chief of staff. If that's not correct, then you'll have to tell your boss there was a misunderstanding because the current arrangements are not at all satisfactory. Another time, perhaps. I'm taking this lady to breakfast."

He stiffened, then glanced around, giving himself time to consider his options. Chea Pran didn't seem to be the sort that would want his minions improvising.

I had a hunch that when it came to alternative courses of action, smacking me in the head and tossing my inert form into the car ranked high on his personal list of favorites. The trouble was, he probably had no idea how important I might be to his boss. "Very well," he said, finally.

The restaurant wasn't far, just a few blocks that we could have walked easily nut Chea Pran's thug seemed content to drive.

He let us out in front. "Second floor," he said. We went in and found Chea Pran waiting at a table on the second-floor balcony, overlooking the sluggish brown flow of the Tonle Sap. He scowled at the sight of Chatty Kathy. "Why is she here?"

"She is my chief of staff, my adviser on local-knowledge things. I don't go anywhere without her."

"And I'm hungry," she said.

Chea Pran made a face and cocked his head at a waiter. We weren't asked what we wanted, but as we sat down at the table the waiter set a place for her and then brought out plenty of food.

Watching Chea Pran's mobile face, my uneasiness about him came back. I wished I hadn't come. Something underneath the surface told me not to trust him. In the daylight, he seemed more self-assured, more confident of his position.

"I have a job for you," he said over coffee.

"I'm not looking for work," I said.

"You were working last night," he said.

"I was playing cards."

He smiled. "But you are a professional player. I want to hire you to play cards."

That surprised me. "That's a new wrinkle."

"Perhaps."

"How does that even work?"

"I provide the stake and the leverage to get you into a high-stakes game. The one I have in mind is tomorrow night."

The idea of playing with someone else's money sounded nice, but it is one of those things that only holds up in fantasies. In the real world, it is just asking for complications.

"If you can afford it, why not play the game yourself?" I was trying to figure out his angle. I certainly couldn't work as a ringer, playing in his stead. Glancing at Chatty Kathy didn't help. She was staring at the waiter and pretending not to soak up every word as she ate her breakfast.

"You are laughing at me."

"No. I'm trying to figure this out."

He waved a hand. "That's all right. It must sound odd. The truth is that I was invited to play. While I like the game, as you well know, I'm not good enough to play with high stakes. I don't mind losing, but I could easily lose too much."

"But you want me to play?"

He nodded. "For me."

"Why?"

"Because of a man who will definitely be in the game."

Something clicked. "You want me to play against someone you don't like?"

He nodded and his eyes rolled up and to the right. I study faces and could tell that the image of a man's face had filled his head.

"A man named Alex. This man thinks that he is a great poker player, but he is just a cheat. Recently, he cheated me and embarrassed me in front of important people. Now, I want him to lose face. I want you to show the other players his foolishness."

The logic of that stunk. "Is it that such big a deal? How will my beating him help you regain face?" I knew a bit about the Asian idea of face, but there were many nuances.

The man's face turned dark and he forced Alex's face out of his head long enough to glare at me. "To me, beating him, having it done, means everything. I owe this Alex payback."

"I see." I nodded, stalling. "But what, exactly, would you expect from an arrangement where I play him with your money? I mean, even if all goes well, you can't be there watching and witness his defeat."

"But the word will go out. The rumors will spread. And besides the satisfaction of arranging it... I will share in his money." He nodded, agreeing with himself. "I provide the buy-in and when you return my investment, you keep half the money you win."

That was the first part of this entire deal that had any appeal at all. "What's the game?"

"Texas Hold'em."

That was good. I held up a finger. "One, important question: What happens if I lose your money?"

"Don't think negatively, Aaron," he said. "You are a professional. You won't lose."

"That doesn't mean —"

"You will win. I have every confidence that you will win."

"So, you will simply hand me the money to play? You trust me?"

The man sat back. "Trust isn't necessary."

I laughed. "Since when?"

He sat back and took out his phone. Before I could react, he snapped my picture. "Before I hand over the money, I will add a photo of your passport to my little album."

"Making a Facebook post, are we?"

He smiled. "For my friends in immigration... people who owe me favors. They'll post it at every checkpoint. It's a small country and there aren't many border crossings or ways out. If you were to steal my money and run, you'd never manage to leave."

"Trust is overrated... especially when you've got tech," I said sourly.

Kathy put a hand on my knee and squeezed it. Probably reminding me not to sass an excellency. Every moment I spent with this man, the less I liked the idea of working this game. Not only didn't I like his strong-arm tactics, but I also had the feeling that he wasn't telling me everything.

"Do we have a deal?"

"Some of this doesn't sound right," I said. "I play a fair game."

He shrugged. "If you can win that way, it's fine with me."

"And what if I can't? This is a challenge you've presented me with. The cards don't always cooperate. Winning honestly could become a problem."

His smile made me shudder. "I doubt it would be as serious or difficult a problem as your imminent deportation."

I stiffened at the threat. "What deportation?"

His attempt to look casual was almost funny — a caricature of feigned indifference.

"If you don't agree to my little scheme, this afternoon immigration will take you into custody based on an anonymous tip. You will be jailed for a time and then deported for violating the terms of your visa. Although I haven't checked, I'm sure you arrived on a tourist visa, and yet you worked last night, playing poker."

"No one gets deported for that."

He smiled. "Unless someone with connections wishes it."

I glanced at Kathy. The look in her eyes told me she was damn sure he wasn't bluffing. I had to bow to her experience. Being jailed in SE Asia was never a good thing. I knew people who'd had the misfortune to experience the hospitality it afforded. "Deported to where?"

His hand waved again, floating across my blurred field vision. "To wherever you arrived from. It will be easy enough for my contacts in immigration to determine that from your files. Then I will ask my people in Malaysia to make inquiries about your activities there. They know other gamblers in Penang and perhaps they can contact some of your friends in the city so they can meet you."

The man was either a cynic who thought the worst of everyone or he had read between the lines and assessed my situation with uncanny accuracy. Either way, the prospect was chilling.

I didn't know what the situation was back in Penang. I'd hoped that if I stayed away long enough things would cool down. But this soon, any inquiries, any suggestion I was on my way back, might stir things up again. A grumpy loser willing to send muscle after me might have a long memory.

In short, being sent back to Penang didn't seem like it would ensure a healthy future for me. Worse it would cost me money for yet more plane tickets. I was losing options. In return for doing his bidding, the man offered me a chance to win the money I needed and avoid deportation.

The situation was exactly what Chatty Kathy anticipated. Excellencies use people, she had said. She thought the challenge lay in figuring out what you could gain from the situation. And there was potential profit in this for me. Besides, I had every reason to believe that if I defied him, he would do exactly what he said.

"I've never tried to target a single player, Prea Chan. Never even considered how it would be done."

That was true. I had trouble imagining how a person would go about that. Trying to win money in a game isn't the same thing as focusing on taking the money from one person. The very existence of other players complicated any strategy I could think of, of course, I wasn't thinking all that clearly.

Che Pran let an impatient hand brush away invisible insects. "No matter. You are skilled and clever. I am certain you can do it. You must do it. I'll give you the money and arrange for your name to be on the guest list."

"But isolating and beating one player—"

"How you manage the task is up to you. But you must clean him out slowly. Don't just take his money but humiliate him. I want you to show the other players how bad a player he is."

"You want him to suffer."

"A few hours into the game they usually take a break. I want you to call me and tell me how it is going. If you can manage without him noticing, send me a picture of him at the game. It will make a nice memento."

I could tell that 'if you can manage' wasn't as optional as it sounded. "That might be tricky. People don't like you to take pictures in those games."

He disregarded my objection. Another invisible insect. "Once we settle up, I'll release the flag on your passport. Then you will be able to leave whenever you want. If you are concerned about Alex, if you fear any repercussions he might decide to rain down on you, then I will take you straight to the airport."

The idea of this Alex character wanting revenge had occurred to me. I doubted going to the airport would help. That the idea seemed to amuse Chea Pran wasn't reassuring.

Regardless, the reality was that Chea Pran didn't need me to agree to his plan. He held all the aces. I agreed. I didn't see a way out. "So where and when do we meet to settle up accounts?"

"When the game ends, go down to the karaoke club. It should still be open. Give me a call and I'll have my man pick you up."

That didn't sound promising either. His man wasn't a friendly type and I couldn't count on Chea Pran and his muscle living up to their end of the bargain. Trust was, in fact, in rather short supply.

As I digested it, he sat back in his chair, watching me, evaluating. "I detest karaoke," I told him.

"You won't be there long. Do I have your word? Are we doing this?"

More than anything I wanted to tell the man to kiss my ass. I didn't like him or his plan. There were too many ways for things to go wrong for me and not enough upside.

On the other hand, he waved a substantial stick. Being thrown in jail would only be unpleasant. I could manage that. But being deported... in the best case, it could affect my ability to get to Singapore. The officials in Singapore didn't look kindly on anyone who had been in trouble.

Worse, if Chea Pran followed through on his threat to put out the word I was being sent back to Penang... that might mean I didn't live long enough to worry about Singapore at all.

I took a long breath. Playing, committing to winning, was also a calculated risk, but I didn't seem to have a choice. "I suppose we do."

Grinning, he reached inside his coat pocket and brought out an envelope, and put it on the table. "Then I need your passport." When I slid it across the table, he took a photo of the front pages with his cell phone.

"Now we are set," he said. He handed me a card with an address written in Khmer. "Here is the address of the game. It starts at nine. Have your..." He grinned broadly, "your chief of staff... that's what you called her, correct?"

"That's the job title."

"Well, have her take you there."

Kathy took the paper. "Here?" The man nodded, and she said something to him in Khmer. He laughed.

"Your whore thinks a fancy game should be held in a nicer place. She's right, of course, but Chan's game isn't authorized by the State, so he takes precautions."

I nodded, feeling numb and helpless. This was not the right way to get into a game. Not even close. I had no idea how to get around the trap he had set out. For the time being, he was in charge. He'd made an offer I knew I should refuse, but couldn't.

When we both stood, he smiled, actually looking happy. "I'm looking forward to this." And then he shook my hand and left.

Kathy and I watched him emerge downstairs. The dark SUV pulled up, and he got in. "He's an excellency," she said sympathetically. "Excellencies get what they want."

That had the ring of a defeatist mantra in the mouths of most people. Kathy just sounded resigned to it.

"He's a thin-skinned, well-connected asshole." Even as I said the words, I realized that somehow the man's very existence, his success, firmly confirmed Chatty Kathy's theories on life.

The idea saddened me and yet spurred me to the only action I could think of — I sat back down, signaled to the waiter, and ordered a whisky. It wasn't even noon, but he didn't even blink. "Chea Pran said to put it on his tab," I said.

That earned me a nod. He was a flunky. He didn't care.

Kathy poured herself more coffee from the pot. She stayed silent, sensing that I needed time to let the reality of the situation sink in, that I would have to accept the way things were.

"I don't know what to do," I told her when I finished my drink.

"Do what he said. You have to go to the game," she'd said. She let her hand creep into my lap. "And now you have to go to your room so we can make boom boom."

It was the best offer I'd gotten all day, so when my hands stopped shaking, we hailed a tuk tuk and I went to make boom boom with my favorite whore so that the day wasn't a total nightmare.

CHAN'S GAME

The next night, after a day spent enjoying my investment in Chatty Kathy's retirement fund and then enjoying a dinner fit for a king, I once again found myself letting Chatty Kathy lead me through the winding back streets of Phnom Penh.

She babbled at me as we walked, staying close to me as we passed the girlie bars where other women offered me encouraging reasons that I should dump her and enter their establishment to buy them a drink.

"You told Chea Pran you didn't like the place we are going," I said. She nodded. "What's wrong with it?"

"Chan has plenty money and the players are rich and his club is a dump," she said flatly, making me laugh.

"You are quite a snob for a bar girl."

When I saw her wounded look, I regretted my words immediately. "You think I'll always do this?" she asked. "I won't always be a bar girl."

"I'm sure you won't," I said. I meant it too. "What do you want to do?"

She let out a breath. "What I will do is make money and be rich."

"How?"

"A girl must be open to various possibilities and taking steps."

"Makes sense, but what kinds of steps?"

She ticked them off on her fingers, bending them backward, nearly to her wrist, the way Khmer girls seem to be able to do.

"A generous excellency might want a new mistress, or I might work as a madam or bar owner or run a front business for one of the many mafias or tongs. There are many ways to make good money and live well."

She knew her world and her options well. I admired that rather than spending her life resenting being born into a dung heap, she simply and matter-of-factly looked for a path that would take her to the top of that heap.

Walking through the noisy chaos, most of it playful teasing arising from an incurable optimism, there were darker sections where a sudden quiet would feel ominous. But Kathy knew the streets well and had a better-honed sense of danger for this situation than I.

I made myself relax. When I did, I found myself relishing the charm of walking through the warm night air, smelling the odors of a strange place. This, I reminded myself, was the essence of foreignness.

One of the fascinating aspects of foreign places, at least for me, is the smells. In a new place, the strange odors, from the smells of street food cooking to the rotting garbage, tend to be obvious at first. They can be delightful or disgusting, but they are new, and they sharpen the sense of being out of place.

I know that feeling unsettles some people, but it comforts travelers like me. A place that smells different promises new experiences, new things to learn and discover.

Unfortunately, those smells become the norm all too quickly, and it is as if you suddenly stop smelling them. Your awareness closes down just a little, and that sense of foreignness begins to ebb. Ask any traveler.

It is such a small thing, the smell of the streets, yet it drives me. I could play poker in almost any country in the world; I could pick a place I like and live well. But once I realized how smells worked, what they did for me, I also understood that regaining that sense of strangeness (being the stranger in a new place) was one of the many things that had kept me moving from place to place, never wanting a home. Or perhaps home was the road. I've heard that said. What it means must vary with the person.

Although the streets Kathy led me through were similar to the ones we'd traveled to Wang's club, when we arrived, climbing stairs that led above a karaoke club, we entered a much nicer place. That boded well for a high-stakes game.

It was cleaner, had a nice table, a well-stocked bar, and most everything you want for a serious game and nothing that might prove a distraction. Distractions are the last thing you want to deal with when you play poker. If you can't focus, it's hard to play your best.

Like Wang, Chan, the man who ran the game was Chinese. Thinner, better dressed, and with good manners, he was an upmarket version of Wang.

When I told him Chea Pran had arranged for me to play, he nodded and held out his hand. I handed him the envelope with the money, and he smiled.

"This is Ann, your dealer," he said introducing me to yet another lovely Khmer woman. Like most Cambodian women, she had the youthful look of a teenager — it seems impossible to guess their ages until they are ancient, and even then, all you can say is they are old. The way Ann handled the cards, and herself for that matter, was experienced. She projected a bearing that was calculated to instill confidence in the players.

At my instruction, Chatty Kathy chatted up the bartender, slipping her some money and explaining my drink order and then bringing us each a drink.

While Chan and Ann arranged things, we watched the other players arrive. Alex turned out to be a big man with an Eastern European accent. He dressed casually, introduced himself with a smile. The man was totally different from what I'd expected. I guess I'd expected a Cambodian who used a Western name, an executive type. Alex had a blue-collar vibe. Not that it mattered.

Soon we sat down to play. As usual, I started off easy, trying to get a feel for the styles and characteristics of the other players' games. I was particularly interested in Alex, of course, but determined not to be obvious about my singular focus.

Initially, Alex struck me as a taciturn guy but watching him interact with people I realized that I had it wrong. He chatted with the dealer and the other players jovially enough. Flashes of humor danced across his hard face.

I sensed that Alex had the rare ability to take things as they came. His face simply reflected that equanimity clearly.

Once the game started, that impression proved even more correct. He played well, trusting his instincts and reason. I hoped his calmness might cover a tendency for bluffing. To test that theory, even when I had garbage hands and I had a hunch he was trying to buy the pot, and the pot was small, I called him even.

That turned out to be a waste of money. That placid face could have been watching paint dry. The only tic I saw was after the hand was over. His surprise at my weak hand barely caused the right side of his face to tighten in a half-smile.

That didn't help me find a tell that would let me know when he was bluffing.

When I took a break, one of the other players did too. He'd been silent at the table, so it surprised me when he introduced himself. "Brigadier General Bona," he said as I came out of the bathroom.

He was standing at the bar, holding out a hand. As I shook it, I took a good look at him, sizing him up. He was a tall, thin Khmer man, with dark eyes. "Brigadier General?"

He chuckled. "Most people take me for an accountant."

"No offense meant, Brigadier," I said. Clearly, he was an excellency.

"None taken. I wanted to meet you. I wished to speak to you."

"Why?"

"Because you seem intent on playing head-to-head with our Alex," he said. The idea seemed to amuse him. "I'm curious as to why that is."

Clearly, this was a close-knit group, and this general was an observant man. The 'our Alex' was the only disturbing, slightly ominous wrinkle.

Although I didn't like hearing that he'd spotted my focus so early on, he was clearly well trained. That made it inevitable and at least we were talking. The conversation had dangerous overtones, but it was friendly. "Is that a bad thing, beating Alex?"

He closed one eye and opened it again. It looked like a slow-motion wink. "Just difficult. I mean it is difficult to win, of course."

"He seems to be a good player."

The general cocked his head. "Good, yes. Most people aren't willing to discover if he can be beaten. Not seriously."

This man was able to make everything sound sinister. "Why?"

"Often people are intimidated by his... line of work."

"I can't be, because I don't know what it is," I said.

He nodded. "I suspected as much. You see, Alex is the local head of the Russian mafia."

"Fuck!" I said. The extent of what Chea Pran had omitted was starting to become clear. I wondered how much else there was to know.

"Exactly," the general said. "Once upon a time the big danger in Kampuchea was the Khmer Rouge. Today it is corrupt officials, through the police, and the mafias."

"I have no interest in trouble with either."

He flashed a thin smile. "If you intend to stay, and intend to engage in illegal gambling, I wish you good luck."

He returned to the table. I hesitated. The twin dangers he'd mentioned were exactly my current problem. Which was the rock and which the hard place, didn't matter, although, in my limited encounters with both, I'd always preferred mafia to corrupt officials. The mafia tended to keep their word.

More importantly, unless Alex decided I was cheating, I was probably safe. It wasn't my first time being in a card game with members of organized crime. My problem would be when he realized that I was less interested in winning in general than beating him. If he noticed and that bothered him, things could get dicey.

And clearly, I hadn't been as suave as I'd thought. The general certainly managed to notice. Alex hadn't given any sign that he did, but he had a damn good poker face.

I took a breath. I couldn't very well just leave. I'd lost some of Chea Pran's money and he'd have me deported. I needed to be very subtle and beat an excellent player without him being aware I was singling him out. I also had to hope the Brigadier didn't mention it.

No sweat.

I got a drink, a real whiskey, a double, and went back to the table for the next hand. When I looked around the table, Alex gave me a cheerful smile. The bastard knew something or thought he did.

It would be a long night at the table. I would play my best... I always did, but I had no idea if I could win the way Chea Pran demanded without cheating. The only thing I was sure of was that I wouldn't cheat. My mother always told me that my honest streak would be my downfall. Chatty Kathy seemed to have the same impression. Whatever, those were the cards I'd been dealt. I'd play them as well as I could.

A FINAL GAMBLE

The game evolved nicely over the evening. A few of the less-experienced players took turns having streaks of winning and losing hands. The few of us who knew the game well taking it in stride, the amateurs getting impatient or overly excited at the rise and fall of their fortunes.

If it hadn't been for my situation, the game would have been incredibly enjoyable. This was my element, my passion. The players were good and the money right.

It seemed that way for Alex as well. He played with a calm good humor that masked a steely disposition, a certain ruthlessness. I admired his ability to chuckle through wins and losses with nothing but a flicker in his eyes giving away his true feelings. He knew his eyes gave him away, and when he felt other emotions, he'd glance down at his cards or pretend to be counting the pot or doing something else to keep us from seeing his eyes.

It was subtle and I doubt most people caught it, but most people don't make their living in the game. As a result, his hiding his eyes served as a wonderful tell in itself. If he raised and looked away, it was a sign to call.

Spotting that tell cheered me, which was a good thing, because the cards I was getting weren't good at all. I'm good, but no amount of skill or practice can turn a pair into three of a kind, no matter how badly you want it. It took all my focus and best effort to stay in the game.

Watching Alex rake in a pot, it dawned on me that when I asked Chea Pran what happened if I lost, he hadn't answered. I had a hunch I knew, and I didn't like my guess.

After a few hours, everyone agreed to a short break. I took advantage of the time to consider the situation.

My clever analysis was that I was in deep shit. I'd lost half of Chea Pran's money. Nights go like that and normally, I'd just write it off to the slings and arrows of outrageous fortune, but I was on a mission.

I'd been right to think playing with an agenda beyond just winning as much as possible was a bad idea. Unless the universe decided to tip slightly to one side, the side that favored me, it didn't seem likely I'd win that money back, much less clean Alex out.

The problem wasn't just that he was a good player, but that there were other decent players in the game too. When Alex had crap cards, inevitably, the way the cards were running, it seemed another of them took over. I was the one out of sync with the game.

I've learned that when things don't feel right, when your gut tells you that you are in the wrong place or time, the best thing to do is quit. Sure, sometimes you can push ahead, keep your eyes open and maybe you can figure out where you put a foot wrong. There might be a path you didn't see, a door you didn't open, couldn't have known about.

Poker can be like that. Most things are like that. But with poker, no matter how much or well you plan, ultimately, the cards decide things, have the last say. In an honest game, no one controls the cards and their power can feel absolute, especially when it's being used against you.

This was one of those times. The pressure of the mission and the bad cards were getting to me and I had started making stupid mistakes.

I was glad for the break.

I went to the bar and got another whisky. As I sipped it, I saw Alex looking at me. He was assessing me, trying to figure me out. I decided to confront his curiosity. I asked the bartender to give me a drink for Alex.

"His usual," I said, then I took it over to him and held it out. I saw his quizzical look. "You are very good at Texas Hold-em," I said.

He took the drink. "You know your way around the table yourself. I expect that with a bit more luck, better cards, you might be formidable."

He scowled. "If I were getting cards like yours, I'd be tempted to call it a night and try again some other time. That you are sticking it out has me wondering why."

He was right. Cutting your losses was the way to go. "I'm afraid this is my one shot at giving you a run for your money."

His eyebrows peaked. "That's a shame. Are you sure you can't come next week? I'd see that Chan invited you back."

"I appreciate that, but I'm leaving the country. I have a visa for Laos where I'm meeting friends."

"So, go meet them. You could come back here afterward. Give me a call and I'll arrange things with Chan and perhaps the cards will be more favorable."

"I'm not sure that's possible, " I said. "If I leave, I'm not sure I'll be able to return."

He raised an eyebrow — just one this time. The other was unmoving. "No? Why is this?"

The question was honest and sounded sincere. Seeing things falling apart, being forced into this situation, I decided to lay it out for him. "When I tell you, you might not want me to come back either."

He smiled. "Now I am really interested in your story. You must tell me."

I shrugged. "It has to do with a gentleman named Chea Pran."

The name earned me a scowl. "He is not a gentleman. He is a cheap crook." Alex put the emphasis on the word 'cheap.'

"He got me my invitation to this game."

A finger touched his nose. "I see."

"He also fronted me the money for the buy-in."

That elicited a flicker of a smile. "The money you are losing is his?"

"Yes."

"I must say that I like that part of your story, but why would he give you money to gamble with?"

"Apparently, you wronged him somehow and I'm supposed to avenge the dishonor."

"Why you? Are you a friend of his?"

I shook my head. "I barely know the man. We met at another game. After I beat him, he contacted me and decided that life would be perfect if I came to this game and took your money."

"Ah." My story made more sense to Alex than to me. "He hoped to regain face. He must think highly of your abilities."

"When we played the other night, he jumped to conclusions about my skill and how much that might matter in terms of ensuring I could win."

"I've noticed that part of his downfall is that he doesn't seem to understand that the cards have a lot to say about winning and losing." Alex sipped his drink, then stared into my eyes. "But you know this. Why did you agree to this foolish and possibly dangerous plan?"

I coughed. "I was forced to leave Penang. Chea Pran knew that or he guessed I didn't want to return. At any rate, he threatened to have me jailed and then deported back there."

Alex nodded. "I believe you. That's his style. But you aren't doing well. In that case, I'm sure he expected you to cheat, and apparently, you haven't done that."

"No. I told him that if I could do it playing fairly, I would break you. I don't cheat. He did, however, make it clear that the terms of our agreement obligated me to win, regardless of what it took."

It was Alex's turn to laugh. "His grievance with me is that I caught him cheating. He was rather obvious. Chan banned him from the game."

"So that is his loss of face."

"That, plus recently I arranged citizenship for some business people of my acquaintance without paying him tea money. He fancies himself as well connected."

"Tea money?"

"A bribe. *Tek tay*, in Khmer." He gave me a hard look. "You've screwed yourself by telling me, you know."

"I was screwed no matter what."

"And I'm sure he flagged your profile in the immigration database. He's a crazy bastard, but he can be thorough. If you tried to leave with his money you'd be arrested."

"That is pretty much what he said. He wanted to save me from the trouble and embarrassment such a misunderstanding might entail."

Alex nodded thoughtfully. "If I were you..." he pursed his lips. "... I'd be thinking of getting on a flight out of the country the first thing in the morning. You might wish to go home now and pack."

I laughed. "And be arrested at the airport before breakfast? Or grabbed from my room tonight? Either way, he'd have me beaten and I'd spend time in jail before being deported and then possibly killed?"

"Not a good option."

"I still have some of his money. You haven't won it all yet. I don't suppose asking you to give it back to him would please him."

Alex waved a hand. "You should keep it. You deserve payment for what he has put you through. Besides, I would imagine that he would consider getting part of it back, and his mission not completed, the same as stealing all of it."

"True enough. Unpleasant, but true."

He cocked his head. "You mentioned going to Laos... I hear it is nice this time of the week."

I sighed. "The two problems with that plan are that I'll never get through immigration and my visa isn't valid for Laos for a few days yet."

Alex nodded. He pulled a business card and a pen from his shirt pocket. He put the card face down on the table and wrote on the back of it, scribbling rapidly in Khmer. He paused to read his work, then signed it with a flourish.

I didn't read Khmer, so when he handed me the card, I looked at the other side. "Kremlin Imports," it said. "Alex Rubbovich, General Manager for SE Asia."

I held up the card and gave him a puzzled look. "And this does what?"

"It solves your first problem. Think of it as an unofficial, but amazingly effective onetime exit visa," he said, his mouth twisting in a self-satisfied grin.

I nodded. "Sweet."

"It's only valid for early tomorrow morning." He nodded toward the table. "There isn't much point in staying to finish this game, so I suggest you go home and pack."

"I can do that, but Prea Chan expects my call at break and to meet after the game. And he knows where I'm staying."

"You are supposed to call him?"

"Yes. He said the group usually takes a longish break late. He wanted me to call and give him a report," I said.

Alex's eyes widened. "Chan!" Then he shouted out some Khmer. Chan and the dealer began clearing the table. The Brigadier nodded and began herding the other players down the stairs.

"What's going on?"

Alex touched my arm. "This is a setup. Chea Pran is arranging a raid. Gambling is illegal, except in casinos and then only for foreigners. That isn't a big deal normally, but some of his friends would be happy to make it sound like no one ever gambled in Phnom Penh before this."

"Shit! What do we do?"

Alex rummaged in his pocket for another card. Fancy Guesthouse, it said. "It isn't far, just over by the Silver Palace. You need to move there right now. Pay in cash and use my name. When you get to your room, book the first morning flight to Bangkok. Stay there until you can go to Laos."

"What about all of you?"

He waved at the empty table. "We are just friends having a night out. While you leave, we will go downstairs for some entertaining karaoke. After you check-in at Fancy, call him and tell him that it's going well and I'm down ten thousand. That should trigger the raid. It will be amusing to watch."

Chan came over and handed me money. "For your chips," he said.

I nodded and waved the first business card Alex had handed me. "How do I use this?"

"Get to the airport early, well before the flight. When you get to the departure area, keep to your right. Go only through the immigration booth on the far-right side... as you face the booths. Only that one. Wait for it if you have to. When you hand the official your passport, make sure the business card is tucked inside next to your visa. I recommend you add a twenty-dollar bill as well."

Bribery was escalating things a bit more than I liked, and this required that I believe Alex wasn't setting me up for something. I found I trusted him a lot more than Chea Pran. "And that's it?"

"That's it. The grubby little man who works there will be delighted to stamp you through regardless of any flags our friend has hoisted. That card will be of more value to him than turning you over to immigration officials and the money will help soothe his conscious, if he has one."

I stared at his face, but I couldn't read it. Was he bluffing? Suddenly, I decided to take everything he said at face value. It was a gut play and there was no logic to it, but his confidence, and everything I'd seen and heard about the influence of the Russian mafia in Cambodia, throughout Asia, made me think he knew what he was talking about. This was golden. "Why are you doing this?"

Chatty Kathy came over and stood beside me, smiling at Alex. In the chaos, her survival sense had kicked into overdrive. She'd helped Ann and Chan clear away any sign of gambling. Now I was sure that she had worked out that I'd be leaving. She was ready to move on and she liked the look of Alex. The woman could smell a serious player a block away.

Alex smiled back at her. "I'm helping both of us. You see, I've decided I like you and admire your directness. Also, I would like to play poker with you again under different circumstances."

"Different circumstances?"

"If I left you to the mercy of Chea Pran, I'm afraid that might not be possible. Besides, your story has prompted me to deal with that insect once and for all. This foolish attempt to entrap me is so typical of the man and his futile power plays... he has been a nuisance for some time. I don't pay him much attention normally, but this I can't ignore. He dares poke the bear." His face lit up, picturing that. "He needs to learn that doing so will get his hand bitten off."

I could imagine Chea Pran if Alex came for him. He'd tremble in fear, his confident facade couldn't hold up against that stare. "You are going to take him down."

"After you are gone."

I was starting to like Alex. "Odd, but now that you mention it, I feel a sudden urge to travel. I'll call our friend later this evening and let him know his arrangements are working out splendidly. You are furious at how badly your evening is going and determined to win your money back. We could be here until morning."

"Excellent."

Alex ordered another drink and turned his attention to Chatty Kathy. When he held out a hand, she moved to him in a flowing, lithe, cat-like drift from my side to his. I recognized it as a definitive statement of a shifted alliance. I winked at her.

"Of course. Leaving this lovely, sassy *shlyukha,* this whore, with me will let you carry out our plan." He gave me a sly grin. "I'll see that she is taken care of properly. Your flight should be early."

"I should get some sleep. Chatty Kathy isn't big on sleeping at night."

"In the morning we sleep," she said.

I left the building and wound my way through the narrow streets until a tuk tuk driver, desperate for a last fare called out to me. He said he knew the guest house I was staying in.

Naturally, he asked for double the fare. I agreed to it. Overpaying was better than getting lost in the winding streets. I gave him the card for Fancy and told him I'd need him to take me there in a few minutes. He scowled, but I knew I was making his night.

On the way to my room, I thought of Kathy. She was landing on her feet and I was glad. I liked her. A lot of whores were just about getting you off for money, but Kathy moved into your life. She'd never be happy as a man's wife, as she preferred being a short-term rental, but she had a good sense of fun. She made me feel that she might actually like me.

The tuk tuk pulled up outside the guesthouse. Three whores were standing around out front. None of them were smiling. This late, they didn't have much chance of finding business. Under other circumstances, it might have been interesting to see if they'd go for a two-for-the price of one deal. But I did need to sleep.

If Alex were telling the truth and I made it through the airport, tomorrow I'd be in Bangkok. Whatever awaited me there, I'd be out of Chea Pran's trap.

FLIGHT PLAN

In action movies, an escape is usually dramatic. The bad guys are in pursuit and the hero makes a dash for freedom. He runs through the traffic of busy streets; he jumps turnstiles and topples vendors' carts to slow his pursuers.

A real escape through an international airport is different. You can't run. You can't even rush things. Jumping or toppling things is right out. In fact, the last thing you want to do is attract any attention at all.

As in the movie, there are heavies with guns everywhere, but some belong. You can't know whose muscle they are until it's too late.

As a result, the tension is internal, not cinematic at all. Your stomach churns with dread while you stand, as if you had nothing better to do, holding your place in packed lines, waiting for permission from armed goons to move forward.

It's a time of torment as well as patience. You are poked and prodded at their whim; you offer yourself to them — as docile as any of the other sheep. You feign indifference as they scrutinize you and your documents, and all the time you are waiting for the moment when it all goes sidewise, the instant they yank you from the herd.

And that's an ordinary departure. Nothing was ordinary this morning. This morning a hasty breakfast lay heavy in my stomach as I went through those motions, walked the multiple gauntlets of human and technological analysis.

Passing through the intense scrutiny, the glares of authorities who might be in the pocket of Prea Chan and all the time trusting my fate to Alex, of the Russian mafia, hoping his good will would protect me… the irony was not lost on me. But it wasn't funny either.

At every moment I expected to be grabbed by the collar and yanked out of line.

"It's you!" some muscled, well-armed thug in uniform would exclaim. Then the others would swarm me and take me prisoner.

My shirt was soaked with sweat and my hands shaking by the time I reached the designated immigration booth on the right-hand side and handed over my damp passport, complete with a twenty-dollar bill and Alex's business card tucked inside.

The promised grubby little man was a chubby little woman, but the sleight-of-hand she performed on those items without the slightest hesitation made it clear I was in the right line. She stamped my passport with a flourish, and then, without a trace of a smile, handed it back and wished me a pleasant flight.

I exited to the gates as quickly as an honest tourist who was not a fugitive would.

I was early for the flight. Waiting is always stressful. For someone who has influential people gunning for them, waiting in a wide-open public place takes the tension to a new level. Fortunately, a vendor at the gate sold cold beer in cans.

I gave a silent thanks to The Powers That Be and bought several.

I drank my beer and stood near the gate facing out, pretending to be interested in the vital work that airport mechanics and logistics people do, or the intricacies of planes, or whatever was out there.

All I saw were pictures of stormtroopers, in my head, fortunately, and a blur of men and women in uniform in my peripheral vision.

Finally, the flight was called. I had bought a first-class ticket and trembled as the attendant checked my passport against my boarding pass and ran the pass through the machine that represented the last chance for officialdom to scream "gotcha!"

I floated down the jetway, found my seat, and slumped into it. A charming Thai lady in an airline uniform offered me a drink. "Please. Whisky, straight up."

I sipped it as the others took their seats. I had passed all the gates, but I was far from free yet.

The engines rumbled to life. A haze of announcements and demonstrations floated around me. The plane moved away from the jetway.

I ached with the tension as the engines revved up, and then the plane began to roll down the runway and launched me to freedom.

"Thank you, Alex," I sighed.

"Sir?" the stewardess asked, her plastic smile firmly in place.

"Can I have a couple of these?" I asked, holding up my glass.

She winked. "Of course."

The drinks, being airborne, all made me relax slightly. I was weak from the tension.

It was time to consider my next moves. I took deep breaths trying to remember if I'd mentioned Laos to Chea Pran. I couldn't remember. I didn't know how connected he was, but if he knew I was headed to Vientiane then I probably needed to change my plans.

I thought of a woman who ran poker games in Bangkok. I'd left her on good terms. She might be willing to let me play. I could stay there, or down in Pattaya. The idea appealed to me. I'd call my friends and tell them things had come up.

If I were gambling in Bangkok, there was no doubt that Alex would be able to find me if he wanted to. The town was lousy with Russians. But I didn't worry about him. Not this time.

Trusting him, trusting that he'd approve of me getting back to work away from whatever he was up to, away from Prea Chan, was a reasonable plan — a calculated gamble.

THE END

ABOUT THE AUTHORS

J. LEE PORTER

J. Lee Porter is a former IT specialist, programmer, and data analyst for banking, security, and government agencies. He left the IT world behind on July 4, 2016, declaring it his personal Independence Day to travel the world full time in search of inspiration for his writing.

Jeff is on Twitter at @JLPorterAuthor
His website is www.nomadicgiant.com

ED TEJA

Ed Teja is a writer, poet, musician, and boat bum. He writes about the places he knows and the people who live in the margins of the world. After being friends with tech giants, pirates, fishermen, and a coterie of strange people for many years, he finds the world an amazing place filled with intriguing, if sometimes crazed, characters.

You can contact Ed on Twitter at @ETeja
His website is www.edteja.com

If you liked this story, please leave a review.